Blindly in

QUARANTINE

L. MOONE

CONTENTS

THIRTEEN DAYS LEFT

Time is a funny old thing. When you're negotiating overcrowded trains, doing your best to keep track of your suitcase as well as your carry-on, and finally rushing through the airport in order to make it to your gate on time for your connecting flight, it passes so quickly, entire hours seem to get lost within the blink of an eye.

And then, when bad weather ensures that that last flight you were counting on gets canceled, and you find yourself stuck in a bland airport hotel, seconds can feel like days. Unfortunately, I have thirteen more days of this drudgery to look forward to, because I've been placed under quarantine.

I thought we were over this kind of crap by now, but hey. A new virus with the potential to cause an outbreak has sent the Paris airport authorities into overdrive. Apparently I may have gotten exposed to a confirmed carrier, whatever that means exactly. I didn't interact with anyone throughout my short stopover at this airport, but they wouldn't listen to my reasoning and now I'm stuck here all alone.

The walls are that kind of off-white which home

makeover shows and real estate agents refer to as 'magnolia'. There is a crack developing in the ceiling, running parallel to the wall. The TV stations on offer are mostly in French, which I don't understand enough of, except for BBC World and CNN, which keep repeating the same three stories over and over again.

There's hardly any news anymore, except the virus threat, which might still just turn into a bag of hot air. Even in the outside world, time is at a standstill.

Meals are served at somewhat regular intervals. But the days pass so slowly that even a five minute delay can test my patience. The windows don't open, and anyway, the room faces a ventilation shaft, so there isn't any view to speak of.

Twice a day the phone rings, and a man with a thick French accent asks me how I'm feeling. I'm fine, and yet, I'm not. It's been days since I've had a sensible conversation with another human being. Still, I tell him everything is okay.

When I was brought here, in the back of a nondescript passenger van driven by a dude clad head to toe in white PPE, it was already dark outside. A few of the windows overlooking the parking were lit up, but most of the hotel looked empty. Forgotten.

I feel sorry for the staff who have to carry on working here for as long as I have to stay. I'm sure they'd much rather be at home with their families.

Safe. That's what I try to focus on; that I'm not so bad off. There are people who aren't getting three square meals a day, and mine arrive freshly cooked at my door. The food's been okay, too, even if I don't have much of an appetite, because I'm doing absolutely nothing all day.

I stare at my phone, with its large crack spread across the otherwise black screen like a lightning rod, as if it'll start working again if I simply look at it with enough conviction.

It doesn't. I'm cut off from everyone I know, even the internet. I knew I should have carried my laptop with me, and yet I'd left it behind, because 'nowadays a phone can do everything, anyway.' I was only planning on being away for a couple of days! Plus, whenever I have my laptop, I'm tempted to catch up on work, and I really needed a break…

This particular phone, however, can't even do the basics anymore. Not even a phone call.

Once I've spent a few minutes mourning its demise for the fifth time today, I stare at the clock. It'll be hours before I get my dinner, left outside my room by a nameless, faceless person who doesn't stick around for me to see. They're very careful about avoiding close contact with other people here. Obviously, COVID taught them exactly how to handle this type of situation.

My eyes wander across the rest of the room, its

decor and furniture so familiar I could draw it from memory by now. Not that I'd ever want to. By the time I get out of here, I'll do my best to forget.

It's eerily quiet. I turn up the volume of the TV, just to silence the constant drone of my brain. Twelve nights and thirteen days to go. I'd be lucky to get eight hours of sleep, which leaves sixteen hours a day to get through. In the mornings at nine there's a yoga program I try to follow, despite not being able to understand a word they're saying. And never having done yoga before.

Some of the channels show movies, but they're always dubbed, so that doesn't provide much entertainment. At eight in the evening, there's the evening news. That leaves fifteen hours, into sixty minutes, into thirteen days. I could probably work out the total without a calculator if I really wanted to, but the number promises to be insurmountably high, so I don't dare to.

I wonder if I'm the only one stuck here. The few lit up windows I'd spotted upon my arrival suggested that there might be more people here, all in the same boat. I wonder where they came from, and how they ended up in this situation. Was there more than one identified carrier? Did anyone else hope to catch the same flight as me? Or did our paths unknowingly cross on the way to other destinations? Maybe they arrived before me and have already left by now? I may never know the answers to any of these questions, but they plague me all the same.

I lie back on the bed and stare at the ceiling some more, but soon grow tired of that and turn onto my side. The hotel phone seems to taunt me with its silence. It won't ring again for another four hours yet, and the only conversation I'll get out if it at that time will be:

"How are you feeling today?"—"I'm fine."

It doesn't even allow me to dial out; I've already tried a few times. But… It should still be functional internally, shouldn't it? What if I could find other people, each cooped up in their own boring rooms?

My inner introvert balks at the idea, and yet…

I take a deep breath and pull the phone toward me. I'd have to dial '0' for the front desk, though I'm sure they won't want to have an idle chat with me, but I could just dial room numbers directly, couldn't I?

I start to methodically go through different numbers. First floor, second floor - where I am, third floor. Rooms one through ten, one after the other. I'm not even sure how many rooms this hotel has on each floor…

Mostly, nobody picks up.

Someone answers in 206, but they can't speak English and get rather irate with me, which almost causes me to give up. Still, I grit my teeth and carry on. I'm so desperate to get a sympathetic voice at the other end, I'm close to tears by now.

Room 309. It rings four, five times. I'm about to hang up again, when I hear a crackle.

"Hello?" a male voice answers.

My heart rate surges. "H-hello?" I stammer. "Do you speak English?"

"Yeah. Who's this?"

I'm so relieved, a big fat tear rolls down my cheek. "Thank God, I thought I was the only one in this godforsaken hotel!"

"It's not so bad, is it? The hotel, I mean." His voice is sympathetic, warm.

I smile through my tears and try to sniffle them back in. "No, I suppose not. I've just been suffering from cabin fever."

"How long have you been here?"

"Two nights." At least I think so. Time seems to have lost all meaning, because I have entirely too much of it to fill.

"Oh dear. And you're losing it already?" Even though he's obviously making fun of me, his voice is still a comfort to me. At this point, I'll even take mockery over silence.

"Actually, I dropped my phone on the way to the airport, so that's dead. And I don't speak French, so the TV hasn't been much help," I complain.

"Ah. That sucks."

"Yeah, it does."

"You're alone?" he asks.

"Unfortunately. You?"

"Same."

There's a pause. I grip the phone tightly and lie back against the pillows again, closing my eyes.

"Where are you from?"

"So old school. The age/sex/location of the telephone age..." he remarks.

I grin. "Just the fact that you're referencing a/s/l dates you quite a bit as well, if you don't mind me saying."

"Me? Pfft. Okay, I'll play. Thirty-five, male, obviously, London."

"Nice! I'm twenty-eight, hopefully obviously female, Edinburgh."

"You don't sound Scottish, or even British."

"I'm not, but it feels like home now. You, however, do sound English."

"Okay. Thanks for the... compliment?"

His reaction makes me laugh out loud. "I suppose it is a compliment. I don't know. I'm just so thrilled someone finally answered the phone in a language I can understand."

"Be honest, how many numbers did you dial before I picked up?" he asks.

"Umm... Promise you won't think I'm pathetic?"

"I will make no such promises."

I quickly work it out in my head. "About twenty-eight."

"You're tenacious!"

"Try, desperate."

"Well, I didn't want to put it quite like that, but yeah, okay. So, the vast selection of quality entertainment on TV isn't doing it for you?"

"As I said, I don't speak French. There's only so much BBC World and CNN you can watch in one day," I lament.

"Can't argue with you there. So… you seriously don't have any sort of tech to pass the time? Or even a book?"

"I was traveling light… All I had was that phone. Until I dropped it and it broke, that is."

"Ouch. That's it, huh? All alone and cut off from the entire world…"

"Yeah, pretty much. I don't even know if my family knows where I am. It all happened so quickly, I didn't get the chance to ask for a phone call."

"Wow, that's…"

"Yeah."

There's a pause on the other end.

"Hey, if you give me the details, I could contact someone for you. Let them know."

That offer nearly has me crying again. "You would do that? That's so sweet of you!"

The only number I remember by heart is my old landline, where my mom still lives, so I give that to him. Smartphones have definitely made us dumber as a species.

"Her English is quite bad, but she should be able to understand if you speak slowly. Unfortunately she doesn't do email or anything."

"Your name?"

"Irina."

"Pretty name."

I start to blush, even though I'm sure he didn't mean anything by it. "Thanks."

On the other end, I hear some rustling noises. "It's dialing," he says.

"What's your name?" I ask.

"Matt."

I find myself growing more and more nervous, almost praying for Mom to answer the phone. Finally, I can hear Matt's voice in the distance.

"Hello, ma'am, I'm calling with a message from your daughter, Irina."

The short exchange continues, with him assuring her repeatedly that I'm fine. "Just a moment, hey how about we put this on speaker, maybe you can talk to each other directly."

Awesome! Why didn't I think of that?

There's a bit of an echo and the volume is very low, but I can hear Mom's voice. We switch over to Polish immediately. Through the barrage of questions coming my way, I try to tell her everything is alright, it's just a precaution, and I'll be here for a couple of weeks before being allowed to go home, while Mom tells me about the news coverage of the situation back home. I try to keep it short, so I don't run up Matt's bill unnecessarily. Within two minutes, it's all over and done with.

"Thanks so much for that, Matt! You're a total lifesaver."

"No big deal. I'm glad I could help."

"Seriously. I had promised her I'd call after reaching home, but obviously that never happened. She's been so worried."

"Ah, all's well that ends well."

We carry on chatting, and the time flies. For the first time in days, I'm smiling so much my face feels a bit stiff. I'm so glad I found him.

Before I know it, the bell rings to signal me that dinner is here.

"Food has arrived," I tell Matt. "Be right back."

"I'm jealous, no sign of mine yet and I'm starving."

"I'd give it to you if you could," I say. "Seriously. We should have dinner together once this is all over."

"Why not. Once this is all over. Oh, my food is here now too. I'll talk to you later."

By now, I'm grinning widely. He wants to talk again!

"Bye, Matt. *Bon appetit.* And that's it. All the

French I know."

"Ha, thanks and same to you. See you later," he says, before hanging up the call. I really wish I could. *See* him.

TEN DAYS LEFT

From that first conversation on, Matt and I chat for at least a couple of hours or more, every single day. We start to open up. Talk about anything and everything. From childhood pets to current interests, as well as favorite foods, books, and movies. I've even memorized how he takes his morning coffee. Extra milk, no sugar.

What else is there to do? TV is dull as anything, and I still don't have any other way of entertaining myself. I've started exercising beyond the half hour of yoga in the morning. Not because I like it, but just to have something to do. Sit-ups, push-ups, planks. I'm starting to understand why prisoners tend to work out so much. It's better than sitting around staring at the walls.

And whenever I am sitting still, I've been utterly obsessed with Matt. Even when we're not talking, I'm continuously thinking of topics or questions to bring up during our next conversation. It's exciting, as well as a concern. Will he grow tired of my constant badgering? And then what will I do to while the days away? I've got ten more to go…

Our conversations have gradually become so casual, a third party listening in might suspect a lot more history between us than there actually is. I'd actually miss him if he stopped talking to me. That's how much he's starting to mean to me.

Maybe it's just been nice to have someone to confide in again, I try to rationalize it to myself. I didn't know how much I was missing that until it started to develop with Matt.

Only a few years ago, I had the perfect tight knit friend circle. Violet, Joyce, and I were roommates as well as besties throughout our time at university. We were inseparable and would spend every single day together, just talking about anything and everything as we went about our routines.

Then the two of them moved away from Edinburgh and we grew apart. Now, everyone has been so wrapped up in their own lives, it's become nearly impossible to get either of them to answer the phone even. When I suggested that they join me on this weekend getaway and relive some of those good old days together, both refused flat-out. No explanation, nothing. They're probably just busy, but it still hurt.

Shit, could it be that I've been feeling lonely even before I found myself stuck in this room? The possibility is making me appreciate Matt all the more.

"Has anyone ever told you you're the nicest guy,

ever?" I ask, after he finishes reading out the headlines from the Guardian's homepage to me.

"Nice guys finish last, haven't you heard?" His pitch has changed slightly.

"Aw, I don't believe that's true."

"Liar. I'm sure you'd pick a bad boy over a nice guy every time; be honest." Evidently I've unknowingly hit a nerve. I remain quiet for a moment. Maybe he's hit a nerve too, because I hate how accurate his assessment is.

"I think my choice in men has been questionable so far. But I'm determined to work on that going forward. Nice guys only, from now on." Nice guys like Matt, maybe? My heart rate surges at the thought.

"Yeah, yeah. Talk is cheap. Seeing is believing."

Again, I desperately wish I *could* see. Matt has been my constant companion for the past few days. During those hours when we talk, as well as when we don't. Even in my dreams he's been there. His voice, anyway. The rest of him is a faceless, substance-less mystery.

In a way that's kind of exciting, if it wasn't also so very frustrating. I'd like to at least have some idea of the person I've been obsessed with. The person I'm starting to grow very fond of.

"How about your taste in women? Have you made better choices than me?"

"My taste in women... Unavailable and out of

reach, mostly."

"I'm taking that as a 'no'." There's a tickle in the pit of my stomach. An urge to steer this conversation into a more exciting direction. It could be boredom, or it could be… Well, we seem compatible enough, as far as I can tell. Never a dull moment or an awkward pause in our daily conversations. That must mean something, right?

"I've been thinking about you a lot these past few days," I say.

"Have you?"

I nod, even though I know he can't see me. "Day and night."

"I've been thinking about you too. It's just this situation we're in, isn't it? It's making us react in ways we normally wouldn't." His tone is light and casual, probably because he's misunderstanding the intention behind my words. Men can be so clueless sometimes.

"Not sure that's entirely it. Matt, tell me; have you ever been in a long distance relationship? Do you believe that love is blind?"

He exhales sharply. "I've been in a couple a few years ago, but they never end well, so… no, not really."

"How so?"

"Expectations are dangerous. Reality never lives up to them." His pitch has changed again. Little by little, I'm starting to pick up on the subtle cues in

Matt's voice that hint at deeper emotions. Right now, I'm guessing I've managed to rip open an old wound. Maybe more than one.

"You can tell me all about it, if you want."

"That's all in the past now." He says that, but I don't think he's being entirely truthful. Could it be that I'm actually able to tell when he's lying, just by listening to the subtle changes in his pitch?

"That might be, but the past shapes our present," I say.

He takes a deep breath and does actually tell me the whole story. A few of them, actually. Internet dating in the so-called 'old days of the net' was obviously quite different to how it is now. By the time I got my first taste of unsupervised internet time as a teen, some of that old world still remained, though things were starting to change already. Chat rooms, message boards, and the like were still around. Everyone was just a screen name; there were no profile pictures. You didn't say hello, you started a conversation with the good old acronym 'a/s/l', meaning age/sex/location. There was no Skype back then, no Facebook, not even its largely forgotten stepsister, MySpace.

You weren't *supposed* to tell people your real identity back then. It was all a great, big secret club, run purely on honor. Sending someone an actual photograph of yourself was something you did only if you really trusted the person you were talking to. Often, such trust turned out to be misplaced.

One of the 'women' Matt had chatted to at the time turned out to be a middle aged man, so obviously that didn't go anywhere. Another, he had exchanged messages and emails with daily for six months prior to that. She ended up ghosting him once he finally sent his picture across, after trying to satisfy himself that she was for real.

But despite these two setbacks, a younger, much more socially awkward Matt was determined not to give up so easily and gave the brave new world of online dating another try. It was supposed to be the trendy new way of doing things, after all.

"I vowed not to make that mistake again," Matt says. "By then I'd fully bought into the idea that there was someone out there for everyone, and online, I'd have an excellent chance of finding my counterpart… From then on, I became more upfront about who I was. I didn't wait so long before showing my face. A year or so down the line, I was certain I'd found the one. We chatted for hours every day. Got along perfectly. Finally, we fixed up a time and place to meet for the first time."

My heart is racing on his behalf. That must have been nerve wracking! "Shit… Then, what happened?"

"I took a train to Manchester, where she lived. Waited for three hours in our agreed meeting spot, before finally boarding a train back to London. By the time I got back home, she'd sent me one last email to say she couldn't go through with it. That she'd seen me waiting at the train station, but the idea of our relationship was all that she wanted; not the reality of it. Never heard from her again after. That was the final straw for me."

"Wow, okay. In that case, I can see where you're coming from," I whisper. I wrap my arms around myself. Too bad I can't wrap them around him instead. Because I know a little of what that feels like. To find out that the people who mean the most to you just suddenly vanish into thin air. The parallels between what happened to Matt and what I experienced with my former besties, Violet and Joyce, aren't lost on me. It's got to be so much worse when a lover does it, though.

"I can't blame them, not really."

"Really? I can," I say. And I do. I'm angry on his behalf.

"We were young and stupid. I know I'm not much of a looker, so that's all there is to it. Whoever thinks love is actually blind has only ever dated attractive people."

The resignation in his voice makes me even sadder. But it also challenges me, because I disagree. I am that person who believes in fairytales. Looks don't matter; at least they shouldn't. What's on the inside is way more important.

"I don't think looks are important at all," I counter. "Character seals the deal."

He laughs, but it sounds hollow. "That's something only beautiful people say."

I want to argue some more, but bite my tongue instead. Could he be right? Would I want to date an ugly man? I'd like to think so, even if my previous boyfriends have all been firmly in the 'conventionally attractive' category. Then again, look how all of that turned out for me! It's only been a few days of talking to Matt and I've shared more meaningful conversations with him than anyone I've ever dated in person.

"Most pretty boys are douchebags, I've found. Only after one thing and disloyal on top of it," I tell him instead. "And the girl who left you waiting at the train station by yourself sounds like she fits in the same category."

He chuckles softly. "Okay, Irina. If you say so."

I sigh loudly, frustrated at the world. He's such a sweet guy. Every single conversation we've had so far has proven it beyond a doubt. He's a catch. No matter what he looks like.

"You know, at night when I go to sleep, I imagine you're in the bed beside me. I put the spare pillow under the covers next to me, so it feels like I'm not alone," I whisper. "Then, I imagine we're still talking at night, in the dark." Maybe not *just* talking.

He pauses for a few seconds before responding. "A single pillow would not be accurate."

I raise an eyebrow. "No? How many would I need?"

He exhales sharply. "Oh, I'd say at least two or three."

I glance over at the bouncy pillow that's lying next to my thigh, just to get a better idea. Is that what he meant by 'not much of a looker'? Did he mean to suggest that his attempts at finding love online failed because he's overweight? Are people really that shallow?

This new snippet of information about Matt does not put me off in the slightest. It would be something new for sure. Exciting. The complete opposite compared to the sorts of guys I've ended up with in the past. Maybe that's why he has more substance to him than my previous partners… literally.

I close my eyes and let my mind wander freely. Oh, the possibilities!

"Height?" I ask.

"Six feet."

Great start.

"Eye and hair color?"

"Brown and also brown."

Dreamy.

"Beard?"

"Yup." Are my ears deceiving me, or can I faintly hear the scratch of him running his hands through it just to make a point? The sound is sending a shiver down my back.

"Nice. I think beards are super sexy." My mind has conjured up an image of a tall, husky, lumberjack-looking man with kind brown eyes. I wonder how accurate it is.

He clears his throat. "Your turn."

I quickly rattle off my own stats. Average build, five-five, blonde hair and green eyes.

"I've been growing a bit of a quarantine beard myself, but it's on my legs rather than my face," I tease.

He laughs out loud. "Thanks for that visual!"

"Not my fault they didn't give me any razors in my room. I was traveling light, remember?" I snuggle back into my pillow with a grin on my lips and let out a content sigh. "Thank you, Matt."

"For?" he asks.

"You've given me something more to think about after we hang up tonight."

My conversations with Matt have gotten even more intense these last few days.

I'm headed for the honeymoon phase, my favorite part of any relationship. Sadly that has also always been where things have gone downhill for me in the past.

If we were together in the same room, I'm certain we wouldn't be doing much talking at all. My feelings for him have deepened, and there's only one way I know how to express all that.

Perhaps it's good then that we're worlds apart right now. I've always had a tendency to go overboard on the physical aspect early on in a relationship and ignore those necessary conversations that create a lasting emotional connection.

But with Matt, I'm getting a lot of the latter. Still, the butterflies in my stomach are multiplying every single day, and I'm literally counting down the minutes before I'm due to call him again.

We *only* talk, obviously. There's literally nothing else to do. He's teaching me more about how to communicate in one week than years spent face-to-face with previous lovers.

He's the sweetest guy, in every possible way. And yet…

After dropping some hints about his appearance a few days ago, he initially seemed surprised that I carried on flirting with him. Thinking about it, perhaps I'm a little surprised too. I've always had a type, whether knowingly or unknowingly. And Matt doesn't sound like he fits into that mold.

But the heart wants what it wants. And right now, I want Matt. Flaws and all. I wonder if he wants me too. He hasn't been forthcoming about his own feelings. Sure, he teases me right back when I initiate it. We've opened up about every possible aspect of our past, and still, he hasn't actually told me how he *really* feels, whereas I've hinted at it, plenty.

This morning, my breakfast arrives at nine sharp, but it's not the same old spread I've grown used to. There's an unexpected addition to my tray of food. A Kindle, wrapped in plastic that smells suspiciously like disinfectant.

Ignoring my food, I carefully unwrap the device and inspect it. It switches on readily; the battery is fully charged. When the home screen comes into view, my heart skips a few beats. "Matt's Kindle" is written across the top. Underneath that there's a vast selection of big name thrillers already preloaded. It's not my usual reading, but certainly better than nothing at all.

Knowing how bored I've been, he had the hotel staff deliver me his Kindle? Who the hell does that? Warmth floods my chest so quickly it brings tears to my eyes. I take a deep breath and tightly hug the device. It's the closest I can get to him right now.

The disinfectant smell is still quite strong. They must have cleaned it very carefully before giving it to me. Too bad. I would have liked to catch some of *his* scent too. Looks like all that will still remain a mystery for now.

What a guy. They say actions speak louder than words, and this particular one is hitting home.

Just like that first day when he offered to call my mom for me, I'm convinced that Matt is the kindest person I've ever come across. What's there not to like?

While I settle back against the pillows with the Kindle, I close my eyes and think.

Now more than ever, I'm certain of how I feel. Love *is* blind. I'm sure of it. I don't care what he looks like. No, strike that, I do care; I just know for sure I'm going to like whatever I see. We've gotten along brilliantly; we share a similar sense of humor as well as a lot of overlap in our tastes. I feel more kinship with him than any other guy I've been with. And those butterflies…

I'm in love. With a man I've never laid eyes on.

I pick up the eReader again, and really savor how my heart flips when I read his name.

A delicious sense of anticipation fills me. Eight days to go, and our quarantine will be over.

Eight days, and I'll see him for the first time. There's no doubt in my mind that it'll go well. Even if Matt looked like Quasimodo, he'll still be my hero. My man. He's won me over with his kindness as well as wit.

Yet, he still gets awkward about it when I flirt with him. Maybe I've just been dancing around the issue too much? He needs to know that I'm serious; it's time to be more overt with my intentions.

Rather than be a tease about it, I'm going to throw caution in the wind today. I'm actually going to seduce him. We're going to have the kind of conversation on the phone today that will stay with him forever. I'll make sure he remembers it long after we've met in person and taken our relationship to the next level. Because I'm certain that that's what this is now. A relationship, not just a fling or a flirtation. My feelings for Matt are as real as they've ever been for anyone. It's about time I show him that.

Today is going to be *all* about him.

I switch on the TV to put on Ye Olde Yoga Program, but it passes me by in a blur. Instead of half-heartedly following along with the poses the teacher is demonstrating like I've done every day so far, I'm planning my next move with Matt.

Not having access to my mobile phone is significantly cramping my style. Rather than rely on exciting visuals to brighten his day, I'm going to have to do it all verbally. If I want to be successful at wooing Matt, I'm going to have to up my phone sex game.

The hotel phone rings, causing me to flinch. I take a deep breath to collect myself before answering in my *sexy voice*.

"Hello?" I breathe.

"Good morning. How is your health?" It's Health Check Guy. Ugh!

I close my eyes and exhale sharply. "Yeah, fine. No symptoms."

"Thank you." *Click*.

My heart is still racing. Jesus. He's only been calling every damn day at the exact same time, and still caught me off guard. Never mind. My plan is still on, just as soon as I finish breakfast and give Health Check Guy a chance to finish checking in with Matt.

A good half hour later, I reach for the receiver again and hold my breath while I dial Matt's room number.

"Morning, Irina," he answers. "How are you?"

I close my eyes and smile. Even though I'm nervous, it still makes me so happy to hear his voice. Ah, sweet, sweet butterflies…

"Morning, Matt."

I try to visualize him sitting there in his room, TV on, maybe his arm folded behind his head while lying back against a few pillows. Warm. Cuddly. Inviting.

What would he be wearing? A pair of those baggy gray sweatpants we all love so much on a guy? Probably. Hopefully.

He's looking at me with those friendly brown eyes of his. There are a few creases etched into his forehead, as though he's surprised to see me staring at him.

"I'm good, but I really wish you were here with me," I say.

There's a subtle change in his breathing. Like a short pause and then a slight increase in tempo.

"Oh yeah? Isn't it time for yoga right now?"

"I fucking hate yoga."

He laughs. The sound makes my chest swell and the corners of my mouth twitch. "Then why do you do it?"

"I didn't today. I'm in the mood for another type of physical activity."

"What's that?"

"Oh, you know... cardio." I roll my eyes at myself. If I want my plan to work out, I'd better hurry the fuck up and start being more obvious with him. "But I didn't want to do it alone."

"No? That's going to be a challenge."

"Nah, it'd be super easy. We wouldn't even have to leave the room. Or… the bed."

He doesn't reply; instead, there's a rustle, and then the muffled sound of his TV stops. I have his attention.

"Remember when I said I've been thinking about you, pretty much constantly?" I ask.

"You've mentioned it."

"I had a dream about you last night which left me… wanting."

Again, his breaths speed up just a little. He clears his throat. It's a nervous tic I've come to expect whenever I become suggestive with him. His awkwardness makes me smile.

"What was in the dream?" he asks. He runs his hand over his chin; I can hear the distinctive scratch of his beard. The sound might be faint, but it's still such a turn on.

"I had gone to bed as usual, hugging the pillows next to me in the bed. When I woke up, the pillows had gone and there you were, sleeping beside me."

"Right."

"I couldn't believe it; finally my wish had come true. When I wrapped my arm around you, you stirred, and pulled me tighter against you. It was the most beautiful feeling. Your body against mine; so warm; skin against skin. I couldn't help myself. I leaned up and kissed your lips, felt the gentle scratch of your beard against my chin. You opened your eyes and smiled, as though you'd been waiting all night for me to do that."

He sighs deeply on the other end of the line. I'm starting to have more of an effect on him. Excellent.

"I slipped my hand underneath your t-shirt, and ran it across your chest. I explored you by touch, first with my fingertips. It must have tickled, grazing my nails lightly across your skin; I could feel the trail of goose bumps right where I'd just touched you. After enjoying another taste of your lips, I lifted the duvet off us and planted kisses all over your neck and down your bare chest..." My turn to sigh, while glimpses of my recurring brown-haired lumberjack fantasy play out in my mind's eye. "Do you like your nipples played with? You seemed to, when I grazed one with my teeth, and took it into my mouth and sucked on it... You groaned and fisted my hair."

"Oh God," Matt growls. "Then what happened?"

"I could tell you wanted me to do more with my mouth. I got up on all fours beside you, and carried on making my way downward. It tickled again when I nibbled at the soft skin on your stomach, beside your belly button. You twitched and squirmed a little. I paused only for a second, then slipped my hand into your shorts. You were rock hard for me already. Just how I like it."

"Hell yes, I am." I can hear a crack in his voice.

He *is* aroused. His instant switch from past to present tense makes me smile.

"I wrap my fingers around your shaft. It doesn't give way when I give it a squeeze; it's so firm and thick. But I know what you really want is my mouth. So I pull the shorts down and move in for my first taste. I lick the head of your dick, getting it all wet and slippery before enclosing it with my lips and giving it a quick suck."

"Ohh!"

"Your hand is on my head again, urging me to carry on. That was the plan all along, anyway. I want to please you so bad. I try to take your whole dick into my mouth, all the way into my throat. It's not easy, but I manage it after a couple of tries. I suck harder, and your whole body seems to tighten when I swish my tongue over the tip."

"Baby, then what do you do?" Matt's voice is raw. Every time I close my eyes, I can see him, or at least my imaginary version of him, with his hand down his track pants, fisting his cock.

"Tell me, how hard are you for me right now?" I ask.

"Ready to burst."

I slip my own hand into the waistband of my pajamas and start to tease myself.

"We can't have that, Matt. I don't want our first experience to end so soon," I say. "So I pull back and just tease the tip of your dick with my tongue, flicking it lightly."

"Oh yes!"

"I'm so wet for you! Will you let me ride that thick cock of yours?" I plead.

"Oh god, anything you want."

"I want to please you, Matt. I want to make you feel like a king. Because that's what you are."

"Fuck, Irina." His breaths are short, shallow. His voice sounds strained and unlike anything I've heard over the phone so far. I love it.

"Are you pumping it for me, Matt? Are you ready for me?"

"I am."

"I take my panties off for you. Will you rip my shirt off? I want you to see how excited you are for this."

"It's already in shreds on the floor."

"I climb on top of you and rub my wet pussy against your cock, though it's already slick from my saliva. You can't take your eyes off me, off my naked tits. My nipples are so, so hard for you…"

"I can't. You're beautiful. Everything about you——
"

"As are you, Matt. I want you. I need to feel your fat cock in me, filling me up."

"Then take it. It's yours."

"I know it is. You're all mine right now. I lower

myself down on top of your dick. It takes some coaxing; I'm super tight. But I keep going until you're buried deep inside of me where you belong."

"Oh my god, I can't take it much longer." On the other end of the line, I can hear repetitive rustling. He's at it for sure. I love it.

"Wait for me, Matt. I want us to cum together." I slip my finger in between my slick folds, exerting extra pressure along the soft, smooth skin between my opening and my clit. I'm so far gone, if I rub it hard a few times, I'll be done for.

"Me too." He huffs. "I want that too!"

"I'm so wet for you. Even though it's super tight, your cock slips in and out of me with more ease now. I speed up, and ride you harder. Every time I slam down on top of you, you're balls deep inside of me, just how I like it. Do you like that too?"

"Oh yeah. I love it." Matt groans.

It sends shivers down my spine. I finger myself harder and faster to match the rhythm of our imaginary encounter.

"I steady myself with both hands on your chest and carry on. Faster. Harder! It burns, Matt! It burns so deliciously how you stretch me out!"

"I hold onto your hips as you bounce up and down on top of me."

"You're the best, Matt. It's so sexy how you look at me. I carry on riding you hard, and lean down to kiss you again. I don't ever want to stop kissing you."

"I could eat you up, Irina."

"I want you to suck on my tits, Matt. Will you do that for me?"

"Your wish is my command."

There it is. The first glimmer of my impending orgasm. I wish I could see how far along he is. I wish I could look into his lust-drunk eyes. Watch his right hand pounding away at his cock until it explodes. They say women aren't that visual, but I could kill for a jerk-off video right now. As long as it's him. As long as it's just for me.

"Do it. Harder. I hang onto your shoulder, and keep on fucking you until it hurts. I'm going to give you the ride of your life."

"Oh, you are. You already are." His voice sounds more choked. He's close. He's got to be.

"Oh God! I'm going to cum, Matt. Will you join me?" I cry out, while clenching my thighs together, trapping my squirming hand in between.

"Oh yes. God yes!"

"Fill me up with your cum, Matt! I want you to shoot your load deep into me!"

"Yes, baby!" He starts panting, as do I.

I imagine droplets of sweat on his brow. Cheeks flushed red with pleasure. His head tilting back against the pillow as he closes his eyes in concentration.

"Cum for me," I whisper. "Baby, please cum for me right now."

He groans louder, and the rustling, which had so far been quite intense, suddenly stops as he gasps for air. I cry out his name while my own orgasm washes over me.

"Oh, Matt!" That's all I can manage, before I'm reduced to desperate moans.

I'm incapacitated for a minute or so. With my eyes shut, I listen to his ragged breaths while trying to catch my own. Neither of us speaks a word; not yet.

"Matt," I whisper, once my heartbeat has slowed to a more manageable pace.

"Yeah?" He clears his throat. It's quite endearing that he's still nervous after everything we just did.

"I can't wait until we do that for real," I say.

"Me too."

"Oh, and thanks for the Kindle. I love it." I sink back into the pillows, with a content smile playing on my lips. *I love you.*

Because this is the moment I realize we're on the same page after all. What I feel, he feels too. All this attraction; all this tension. It isn't just one-sided. Perhaps he's just been too much of a proper Englishman to make a move on me. But now, we've taken the first step together. There's nothing more standing in our way.

Our daily conversations have shifted. We still *converse*, of course. But we do a lot more as well. At least twice a day we talk dirty and get each other off. From imaginary blow jobs, we've moved on to every possible position we can come up with. We're exploring everything we can, making the most of our changed dynamic over the phone.

And it's not just me anymore. Not just *my* idea.

Once or twice he's called me at midnight, already breathless, already heading for release and desperate to hear my voice while he takes matters into his own hands. It's such a turn-on to know how much he wants me, physically as well as emotionally. Because I want him equally.

I'm a very physical person, especially when I'm in a relationship. Especially when I feel so strongly for someone, it's the only way I know how to express myself. And by now my feelings for Matt have exceeded anything I've experienced in the past. Perhaps it's the anticipation, being made to wait before we can truly *live* our love.

I can't wait for this stupid quarantine to be over,

so we can take things to the next level.

Just how it's going to work, I'm not really sure though. With me in Edinburgh, and him in London, it's going to be logistically difficult to spend a lot of time together. Especially because this unplanned two week stopover will have maxed out my vacation allowance for the year. Then again, I don't even know what's going to happen after they let us out of here. We missed our original flights because of this mess, so will they automatically rebook us on a new one?

It's been a recurring fantasy of mine to imagine that we'd still be here, in this hotel, endlessly waiting for our flights. But we'd be together in one room instead of apart. Our refuge away from the world, far away from the mundane reality of jobs and bills and household chores. A chance to experience everything we've been missing so far. In my fantasy, our departure date never arrives and we remain here in limbo. Together forever.

But that's a dream, and this is reality. What will really happen? I guess I have to wait and find out.

It's been five days since his Kindle first arrived in my room. During one of our non-sexual conversations, Matt briefly explained how to use the inbuilt web browser for email, social media, and whatnot, and now I'm caught up on all my communications with work and friends. I got it out of the way quickly, so I could free up the rest of my days for Matt. We have just three nights to go before the end of our stay in this place.

While checking my email over breakfast, just as he taught me to, I find a communication from the airline with options to rebook my missed flight. I follow the link and see there's a flight to London Gatwick scheduled for the exact afternoon after our quarantine ends.

I quickly give Matt a call to pass along the details.

"This is great, Irina! Perfect timing."

I nod. "Gatwick works for you, right? Not too far away?"

"Gatwick's good. I can make it home by train quite easily."

"It says to call for other destinations."

"Want me to phone them for you? Find out about any flights to Edinburgh?"

He's being attentive and helpful as usual. My hero. "That would be wonderful."

But actually, the prospect of both of us flying home separately is putting a damper on my mood. He still wants to meet the moment we're released, right? Just as we've discussed?

"Thank you, Matt."

"No problem."

I sigh. "It's actually coming to an end, isn't it? Our quarantine."

"Sounds like it."

"Obviously I should be relieved, and yet…"

He pauses for a moment. "Yeah, I know. I've gotten used to the situation as well now. But we could still call each other to talk every day? If that's what you want."

That's not what I want. Far from it. I bite my lip. But at least it's something. Some admission that he also doesn't want to let go of what we found together.

"Part of me wants to stay," I admit.

"Don't be silly. You've been waiting to get out of here from the moment they put you into this hotel."

"True, but…"

"Tell you what. I'm going to call up that helpline number and get the details for you. You'll want to get back to your life; your friends, as well as your job."

Do I? What friends? Ever since Violet and Joyce moved away, I've been focusing on building my career for the most part. And I have a social life, sure, but they're acquaintances, not what I'd call true friends. Actual friends would have warned me of the red flags, rather than egging me on into the few failed relationships I've had recently. And while my recent promotion felt like the most meaningful thing in the world to me when it happened, now…

Come to think of it, I have very little to look forward to at home. Except what's right here. Right now. With Matt.

"Thank you," I say. I'm not sure I mean it, and yet

I can't bring myself to open my mouth and say what I really think. It's too raw, too risky. What if I freak him out? What if he doesn't feel the same way?

He asks me for my full information, including passport number, just in case. I supply all of it on autopilot while my mind is already elsewhere.

"I'll let you know," he says.

"You're the best, Matt." He is. He's also the worst. Why can't he read my mind right now? Why doesn't he instinctively know what I want? It's not too much to ask, is it? A crazy romantic declaration of love... Telling me he doesn't want to go home without me... Any of that would do!

"Only trying to help," he says. He hangs up our call, leaving me confused and conflicted.

I have to go home sometime, don't I? There have been emails from my job telling me I am to report as soon as I have access to a proper laptop again, that my position is remote for the foreseeable future, except for the occasional meeting at the office. If that's all it takes, a laptop and a proper internet connection, then it doesn't really matter *where* I am, does it? I could be here in this hotel. Or back in Poland with my mom. Anywhere will do, as long as I can travel to the office to attend the occasional team meeting. Edinburgh is pretty well connected, so the options are endless!

The thing is, right now I only want to be in one

place in the whole world: wherever Matt is. And yet he's one floor up in his room, trying to arrange a flight to Edinburgh for me, while booking himself onto the Gatwick flight. I want to spend time with *him*, dammit! *In person*, not over the phone. I should call him back and stop him, but I'm too much of a chicken shit. Weird, how much easier it felt to try and seduce him over the phone, rather than speak my mind now.

He calls back an hour later with the news that indeed, there's going to be a flight to Edinburgh a few hours after the Gatwick one mentioned in the email. My mood hasn't improved much throughout the wait, and now it's even worse. That wouldn't give us much time together at all before his flight. And then what? We'd be apart all over again.

It won't do. I hate this.

"I confirmed it for you," he says. "They needed to know right then and there over the phone. Seats were super limited, so they had to upgrade your ticket to secure a spot."

I don't know what to say. He actually just went ahead and booked my ticket for me. He didn't need to. He shouldn't have! I don't even want to take that damn flight!

"Wow, okay. I'll send you the money for it as soon as I can get into my internet banking again," I stammer.

"Ah, don't worry about it." Matt pauses, and all I can hear is the furious thump of my heartbeat. "Are you okay? You don't sound happy."

"Yeah, I'm just—Thank you so much for helping me with this. I don't know what I would have done without you." I pinch the bridge of my nose in an attempt to calm down. He's trying to help, bless him. But my heart isn't cooperating with this otherwise very sensible plan. My heart is freaking the fuck out.

"It's not a problem. Anything for you, Irina."

Seriously? *Anything?*

"Do you know what the plan is, anyway? Are they going to drive everyone to the airport at the same time, or…?" I wonder aloud.

Matt clears his throat before answering. "You know, I have no idea."

"Guess I'll try to ask Health Check Guy when he calls next."

"Yeah. Me too." Matt's voice sounds weirdly flat.

Our time here is ending, and it already feels like the distance between us is growing. Or is that just my own separation anxiety, rearing its ugly head?

DAY ZERO

We talked every day, except today. D-Day. It's late morning, and I've just finished packing when reception calls. The late morning airport pickup—the one both of us opted for—is waiting outside. Then the buzzer on my door goes off, and a bored looking boy in his late teens or early twenties appears.

He collects my luggage and I follow him downstairs. It's our moment of truth.

Is Matt already waiting? Or is he still on the way down from the third floor?

There's nobody else in the lobby, except the receptionist, who's totally fixated on her computer screen, a middle-aged man with a mustache, and the lad, who's dragging my suitcase out of the lobby and lifting it into the back of the van waiting outside.

"Okay, please, airport," the older man, presumably our driver, gestures at me to go outside to the minivan. I'm confused. Am I the only one here? Where the hell is Matt?

I turn towards the receptionist. "Excuse me. Where is Matt from room 309?" I ask.

She looks at me blankly and shrugs nonchalantly.

"Maybe… Taking the taxi later on?"

I shake my head. "No. He's on the flight to Gatwick at two pm. The later cab would be too late."

She purses her lips and shrugs again. "No other passengers coming now. Only you."

Fuck.

Fuck fuck fuck.

The driver gestures at me again, this time mute. Wonder what the damn rush is, if I'm his only fare. What the actual fuck. Has Matt already left? Without even saying goodbye?

I have no choice but to fall in line and do as I'm told. And I'm reeling.

What the hell has he done? After everything we talked about?

I take a deep breath, hold it for a couple of seconds and let it out slowly. Then, I close my eyes and do it again. Maybe something went wrong. Yes. There must have been some miscommunication. Maybe he thought I was taking an earlier cab as well and—

That's bullshit, though. Because we talked through the details of our schedule every day since we found out the airport shuttle timings.

That leaves only one possibility. He never intended for us to meet.

I open my eyes and watch the non-descript hangars pass me by on the way to the airport. He never planned to meet me. Despite everything we talked about. Despite how close I thought we'd become.

Was it all just a game to him?

'Expectations are dangerous,' he'd told me around a week ago, when we first started to flirt. 'Reality never lives up to them.'

Reality isn't living up to my expectations right now, that's for sure.

When he said long distance relationships never work out anyway, was he speaking from experience, or self-snitching his intentions for the future? Maybe a bit of both.

Maybe this is revenge, for all the women who came before, who let him down in a similar way? What a fucking asshole! When I look down at my hands in my lap, I notice I'm clenching my fists in anger. Ugh. I'm so pissed off, I could scream. But also, so hurt, so shattered, so utterly confused.

Because I can't reconcile this moment with everything else that happened between us. The kindness he showed me over the phone. The fact that he paid for my damn upgrade, no strings attached. He didn't even seem to want me to repay him; I just naturally offered it because he shouldn't have to spend money on me. The Kindle eReader, which I've carefully stowed in my hand luggage, waiting to be handed back to him in person. He clearly wasn't expecting to get it back, considering he's nowhere to be found today.

He did all those things, seemingly without any expectation of reciprocity. And he still stood me up just now? Am I really that unlikeable that people just drop me when things get a little inconvenient? First Violet and Joyce, and now… *Ugh!*

This all makes very little sense. Unless…

Unless his actions weren't malicious. Unless there's some other explanation after all.

I take a few more deep breaths, trying to calm my racing thoughts. Only just in time, it turns out, because right at that moment, my cab pulls up at the Departure terminal.

***

White male in his mid-thirties. Six feet tall and overweight, brown hair and matching beard. There's a disconnect between his description of himself and reality, even if a subjective one. 'Not much of a looker,' he'd said. Yet the man standing in front of me is rather handsome, in a boy next door sort of way. Frustratingly, the cuddly lumberjack fantasy I'd conjured up for myself actually turned out to be pretty accurate.

After how negatively he described himself, my observations are giving me pause. Definitely not my usual type, and yet I'm floored. The resulting tickle in my stomach and flutter in my chest is also making it impossible to stay as enraged as I have been throughout my cab ride here, as well as the insane queues through check in.

It has to be him, though. Nobody else even remotely fits in this crowd of passengers waiting for the Gatwick flight. He's standing off to the side of the spaced out crowd waiting at the gate. Headphones on, eyes fixated on the ground, as though he's doing his best to disappear, even if that would be quite a feat for someone of his stature.

The man couldn't blend into a crowd if he wanted to; in among the few elderly couples and business professionals waiting to get back to London, Matt stands out. For the two of us, this airport was just an unforeseen stopover on a much longer journey. Lost souls, we are. Uncomfortable and out of place.

My heart is racing faster than it ever has. I'm terrified, but I haven't left myself another way out. I *have* to confront him, to figure out if the huge chance I'm taking will blow up in my face some more.

"Matt?" I say.

He reluctantly looks up, eyes widening in recognition when our gaze first meets. I'm enamored by his soft yet masculine features. He's gorgeous up close. I'd be head over heels by now, if only he hadn't hurt me so.

My heart was already heavy, but now it's

unbearably so. Perhaps I shouldn't have done this. Perhaps I should have just left things as they were and waited for the flight to Edinburgh, rather than chasing down this impossible dream and risking further heartache in the process. But I was just too terrified that I'd never find out the truth then.

I have so much to say, and none of it can be done over a phone call anymore. If I don't take a stand for what I believe in, then who the fuck will?

"Irina?" His expression is tense; I can't read it very well.

"You just left," I whisper. "Without even saying goodbye?"

He sighs and looks down at the floor between us. "I couldn't—"

That voice. That voice that has carried me through two fucking weeks of isolation; it brings tears to my eyes again now, but not in a good way.

"As if none of it even mattered?" My chest feels empty. I don't know whether I'm angry, sad, or just deflated. Probably it's a combination of all three. I want to kick and scream and cry, but I keep it together, except for the tremble in my hands.

"I…" He sighs and shakes his head. "I didn't want things to get awkward between us."

"It was always going to be awkward. You just didn't want to face me, it seems."

"Bloody hell. I'm so sorry," he stammers.

"Are you? Then why'd you do it?" I ask.

Why, indeed? Everything he'd done up to the point he abandoned me at the hotel suggested he was looking out for me. It started with him calling my mom for me, before we even knew each other. Then, he gave me his Kindle. Only a few days ago, he arranged and even paid for my ticket home. He was my rock throughout our stay in quarantine. Always a sympathetic ear. Always cheerful and supportive and perfect. What changed?

After we spent hours every day, sharing our deepest, darkest thoughts, things we'd never expressed to another living soul, I thought I *knew* him. Was it all just an illusion?

"I never meant to hurt you."

His words, although they might be sincere, sound hollow to me. The road to hell is paved with good intentions, as they say.

I make a face. "You didn't want to hurt me; you just didn't want to meet either. That's just grand, Matt."

"We were living in a different world these past couple of weeks. We were thrust together by chance."

"So? Is that all it was? Just something to pass the time with and it's over now?"

He sighs and shakes his head.

"Look at me at least," I snap.

My eyes are annoyingly moist now, and when he

looks up again I see that his are too. What the hell is he playing at? He had a whole lot of opinions about love and relationships over the phone, always just spoke his mind. And now he hasn't got the balls to reject me to my face?

"Not exactly," he says. His voice is dull. He barely sounds like himself, and yet I know exactly what this is. He's suffering. But, why? He's the one who hurt me, not the other way around! I've been nothing but honest and genuine.

"Then, why?" I plead. God, I'm pathetic. Have I no pride? I'm standing here in a crowded airport terminal, making a fool of myself in front of a guy who blew me off. Can't I just take the 'L' and move on?

"It was a self-preservation thing. This sort of situation just never ends well."

Again with the fatalist bullshit. Has he learned nothing the past couple of weeks?

"After everything we've talked about. I thought I knew you. And yet I have no idea what the fuck just happened. Help me out here, Matt!" I urge.

He cocks his head to the side. Yep, he's definitely about to break and trying very hard not to.

I'm still angry and yet it hurts my heart to see him like this. Because despite all this shit, I can't suddenly stop caring about him.

"Irina. I know you think I helped you back there.

But it was always the other way around. You have a life to get back to in Edinburgh, just as I have mine in London. Is it not better we part ways now, rather than drag this on until we inevitably lose touch once we're back home? You don't owe me anything."

"The fuck are you talking about?" I snap. A few white-haired heads turn in our direction. I take a deep breath and try to calm myself, but it's barely working.

Meanwhile, he turns red in the face as well and folds his arms. "Okay, you know what? I tried to do this gracefully, but apparently—"

"There's nothing graceful about ghosting me. I thought you of all people should understand that! I thought I meant something to you."

"Damnit, Irina! You mean *everything* to me."

I choke on my own breath and just stare at him. My heart is still beating so fast, it's making me feel faint.

"But this thing between us, it's not going to work," he adds.

"Why not?" I demand.

"Bloody hell, I just explained why. You've got your life to get back to, I have mine. Maybe we'll talk over the next few weeks or months, even. Maybe we'll plan a couple of visits and even spend some time together during the holidays. But eventually, we'll drift apart and get distracted by our everyday lives and…"

"Is that why you did this? Because you think you'll grow tired of me once you get back to your daily routine?"

"Me? No, I—" Matt stammers.

"Oh, so you think I'm so vapid that *I'll* dump *you* the second I get distracted? Be honest. It's the least you can do," I rant.

"Jesus Christ." He sighs and shakes his head. "Frankly? Yes. I think you're a beautiful young woman, with an exciting career and social life back home… You have a whole life to go back to which doesn't include… me."

As hurt as I am, he looks worse. Maybe I've been barking up the wrong tree from the start.

Our entire relationship so far was initiated by me. From the first phone call on, I was the driving force. I decided when to talk, what to talk about, when to flirt… Every damn thing has been my choice and he's been all too happy to accommodate me. But now, for whatever reason, he's choosing to back down rather than move ahead. And there's not a damn thing I can do about it. I can only say my bit and get on with life.

"You may think that all of this was just meaningless, but for me, that's not the case," I say. "For me… You meant something to me. You meant everything to me these past couple of weeks. Which is why it shattered me to find that you'd just left." I fold my arms and hold my breath. Suddenly the air around us feels deathly cold and I'm exposed. Like my words have ripped open a gaping chasm in my chest and it's up to him to close it back up.

He looks down to me again. I turn away to avoid his gaze and find an aged couple about nine feet away flat-out staring at the two of us. I try to ignore them and focus on Matt again. He makes me feel tiny and insignificant, towering over me like that. And I don't like it one bit. Over the phone, I held the reins, and now, I'm defenseless in front of him.

"And if you're not interested in me, just look me in the eye and say so. I'll be okay. Eventually."

The silence between us is deafening, until he nervously clears his throat.

"Of course I'm interested. Fuck," Matt whispers. "I just don't know how to do this."

I hadn't even realized I was holding my breath until I breathe a deep sigh of relief. I'm trying my best here. Trying to remember every conversation; all the stories he's told. Every embarrassing anecdote. Every piece of his true self he's shared with me. I can't believe it was all a lie. And what I'm seeing right now isn't a lie either.

"I'm truly sorry, Irina," he says. "I really never meant to hurt you."

"I'll be honest; you fucked up," I say. "Because I *am* hurt."

He presses his lips together and looks away again.

"Oh God, you obviously love him, and he loves you. Will you kids just kiss and make up already? I can't take much more of this!" a female voice blurts out.

It's the elderly woman who has evidently been listening in for a while now. Her husband puts his hand on her back as if to usher her away from us. She stands her ground defiantly, with her arms folded.

I glare at her, tempted to tell her to mind her own business. But annoyingly, I know she has a point. Even if hearing her mention of the word 'love' made me want to jump out of my own skin. We're just dragging this out, making a scene in front of all the other passengers for no good reason. It's time to speak freely, in private.

"Let's take a walk," I say.

"The flight—" he stammers.

"Boarding won't start for another half hour."

He nods and follows me away from the waiting crowd. We turn a couple of corners and find ourselves alone at an empty gate. Finally, I turn to face him again. My mind is swirling with all the memories of all the conversations we had leading up to today. All the promises I thought we'd made. How did I end up with such grand expectations? It wasn't *all* in my head, was it? For fuck's sake he literally just said he was interested as well. He's still sending me mixed signals!

"What really happened between us, Matt? What did I miss?" I ask, finally.

He sighs and shakes his head.

"I…"

I wait, because it's his turn now. His turn to talk and explain himself. I vow to hear him out without interjecting or trying to steer the conversation anymore.

"Last night, after we'd fantasized together about how our first meeting would go today, I couldn't sleep…" He pauses to clear his throat. Like he always does when he's nervous about what he's about to say. "So, I…" Matt tilts his head to the side and briefly makes eye contact with me, before continuing to stare at the floor. "I kinda cheated… I googled you."

I raise my eyebrows. Well, that finally makes some sense. He had my full name, since I gave him all my details for the flight tickets. A cold shiver passes through my whole body.

"And you didn't like what you saw," I conclude.

"What? No! That's when I realized how much trouble I was in!" he counters.

I shake my head. "I don't get it."

"I'd suspected it from our conversations already, but it didn't sink in until last night. Just how comically mismatched we are. I knew then that there was absolutely no chance—"

"Excuse me?! You saw a couple of pictures of me

and—" That's it, all good intentions out of the window. I guess I am interrupting him after all.

"I had to protect myself. I had to, because—"

"You just decided that we weren't going to work out, based on my fucking *picture?*"I rant.

"Because I knew how much I loved you already, just from afar. I knew—"

"That's hella shallow, Matt!" I snap.

"If I saw you, and then lost you after, I'd never recover…"

I stare at him. He stares back. And I'm still angry. And upset. And—holy shit, did he just tell me he loves me? What the actual fuck did he just say after I started yelling?

My heart is racing so hard, I'm certain he can hear it too, echoing all around us.

"I…" I stammer.

He doesn't say anything; he's just standing in front of me, with his hands stuffed deeply into the pockets of his baggy jeans, looking deflated and vulnerable. And for a change, I'm the one who's lost for words.

He said he loves me. And I… Well, I obviously love him too; I've known it pretty much from the beginning, even if I couldn't bring myself to spell it out. I should do what the annoying old lady said and get over myself already. Everyone deserves a second chance, right? Especially the man I love?

"I love you too, Matt." My chest feels lighter the

moment I say it. Or rather, the moment I see the disarmed expression on his face. Fuck. This is what was missing. I'd never actually told him how I really felt!

He exhales sharply. "This… This is exactly what I was afraid of."

Arrrrgh! How does he continue to infuriate me, just when I find it in myself to calm back down? I close my eyes and take a deep breath to contain my frustration. "Why's that?"

"You think my worst case scenario for today was that you'd see me and reject me, right?"

Well yeah! I nod.

"It wasn't. It was that we'd meet, and everything would seem fine, and you'd give me hope, and I'd fall for it, and I'd get everything I dreamed about—"

"That makes literally no sense," I grumble under my breath.

"And then, when I'd least expect it, probably once we're both back home and settled into our normal routines… That's when I'd lose it all. I'd pick up the phone to talk to you, and you'd make an excuse not to answer. I'd suggest a weekend getaway, and you'd always be busy…"

I shrug nonchalantly, even though this more detailed explanation of his cuts me deep. Because it does make sense. Remembering all the stories of his failed distance relationship experiences, everything falls perfectly into place. For the first time since confronting him, I'm grateful to have a trump card up my sleeve. Maybe I didn't completely mess up today.

"In that case, it's probably a good thing that I'm not going home today," I say.

His head snaps in my direction. "You're not? But your flight leaves in three hours…"

I grimace awkwardly. "I… kinda asked the airline to rebook me onto your flight. To Gatwick. That's why it took me so long to get to the gate."

He opens his mouth, but then closes it again without saying anything. He looks adorable when he's confused, actually.

"I'm… in the seat next to yours," I whisper, holding up my old school printed boarding pass at him. It's amazing what all you can get done when you're nice to the ground staff…

"Why on earth would you do that?" he asks.

"Look, when I ended up in the hotel lobby all by myself, I couldn't think of any other way out. I had to try. I had to confront you!" When I realized what had happened, I knew I had to react quickly. There was no time to think of a game plan, or to consider the consequences. All I had to cling onto was a glimmer of a farfetched dream.

"You could have called me after we both got home. You could have—" Matt says.

I make a face. That's so… sensible and pedestrian.

So boring! "Where's the romance in that? I had to make a stand! For… us. And I've always been more of a doer than a talker."

Deep down I know how I wanted our meeting to go. I'd hoped beyond hope that perhaps he was forced to leave early, that maybe there was a misunderstanding with the hotel and it wasn't his choice. And we would see each other at the airport, run into each other's arms, and that would be it. The beginning of the rest of our lives, RomCom style.

Definitely naive and potentially quite stupid…

"Seriously? We're on the same flight together?" he asks, the corner of his mouth twitching like maybe, perhaps he's about to crack a smile. I bet his smile is deadly, too. Like the rest of him.

"Yep. Now what?" I ask. "Your move."

"Now what?" he repeats. Matt looks down at me, like he has done throughout our interactions together. But it's different now. Gone is the distrust and even fear. Now, he gazes at me with admiration and tenderness in his eyes. Once again, I feel small in front of him, but also powerful. Because I believe him now. He didn't mean to hurt me; he just needed to protect himself. Just as I needed to protect myself by not saying those all-important words first.

I love you.

"Like what you see?" I ask.

He smiles briefly. It's adorable, just as I knew it

would be, and sends my senses into overdrive again.

"Love what I see."

"Me too," I say.

His bottom lip quivers for a moment. "I expected you to be disappointed."

"That possibility never even crossed my mind. And I'm not. I'm in awe," I say.

"I did however expect to feel exactly as I do right now."

"Which is?" I ask

"The best feeling in the world. Which is why it would destroy me if I lost it." Matt's voice is thoughtful, almost solemn.

"You almost did, by running away. But I've decided to give you a second chance anyway," I tease.

He closes his eyes for a second, then takes a deep breath and opens them again. I will never grow tired of how Matt looks at me. Like I'm the most precious thing in the whole world. Exactly how I feel about him. He slowly and tentatively places his hands on my shoulders.

Even though I can't feel his touch directly against my skin, it still tingles underneath my clothes. Who knew? Who knew that all the attraction I felt for him sight unseen would not only translate to this moment, but actually multiply?

I reciprocate by reaching for his neck, wrapping my arms around it lightly at first. His large hands slip down my shoulder blades and onto my lower back just as I tighten my grasp on him.

Finally, everything's falling into place. Because this is exactly what was supposed to happen today. Reality is back on track, matching those pesky expectations he complained so much about. I guess in our case, they're not so much expectations as anticipation. There's a subtle difference, isn't there?

"So, in about twenty minutes, we're going to board that flight together…" Matt whispers, while running his hand through my hair, pushing a few stubborn strands of it out of my face and staring deeply into my eyes. The tenderness and care with which he touches me takes my breath away, and I can't manage anything more in response than a weak whimper.

"And then, a few hours later… You want to come home with me?" he asks softly.

I blink a couple of times, completely mute now.

Get your act together, woman! Snap out of it!

"I don't know if I mentioned it before, but I only have one bedroom…" he says.

I frown. "It's got a double bed, though, right?"

He smiles again and nods.

"That's perfect, then. Because I wouldn't want to be anywhere else."

"No?"

I shake my head. "It was all I could think about, ever since you confirmed my flight for me. That I couldn't bear to spend any more time away from you," I whisper.

His eyes shut briefly, but then he's making eye contact with me again.

"What about your job? Won't they be upset with you taking more time off?"

"Do you have a laptop I can borrow?"

He nods.

"Then we're all good. My boss is letting me work remotely for a while."

"You've thought of everything, haven't you?" He smiles again.

"Not really, it all sort of fell into place. Almost like this was meant to work out, or something," I tease. "Like, maybe it's fate."

He cups my face in his hands and leans down a little. Feeling his breath against my face makes my knees weak. Good thing I've got his thick, strong arms to steady me.

God, how I want to rush this. I want to kiss him, devour him already. I should be grateful he's taking it easy, or this beautiful moment would be over much too soon. Except... I'm not.

"Irina, will you ever forgive me?"

I can't stand it any longer and tighten my grip on his neck, pulling him down against me. Enough already, like that old lady said. No more dilly-dallying.

"Already have," I tell him, just before our lips

make contact for the very first time.

Electricity zings through my entire being. For the first time in weeks, no years, I feel fully alive. This is it. The moment I've been yearning for.

I hang onto him for dear life, helpless, as well as weightless, while he wraps his arms around me, almost lifting me up against him. My heart seems to flood my body with sensations I wasn't ready for. I've had butterflies in my stomach before, but right now, I have them *everywhere*.

Though I've spent many a night and day imagining what this moment would be like, it still takes my breath away.

He takes my breath away.

Our tongues dance around each other, seeking out the other, while simultaneously shying away from continued contact. As if too much of a good thing will blow our minds. It probably would, because I'm dangerously close to losing it already.

He tastes amazing. And he smells even better.

Scent is a powerful aphrodisiac. Any more of this, and I'll risk forgetting where we are. I want to rip his clothes off, like I told him to do to me, during our first frisky encounter over the phone.

Patience… In a few hours, we'll be alone. All will be revealed. All those promises I made verbally will come to fruition.

"I love you, Matt," I mumble against his lips.

I've never said that to anyone before. I mean okay, I've said it to Joyce and Violet many times in the past, but as friends. This is different. This is a first.

I can feel him smile in response. "I love you too," he says.

"No. I love you!" I urge, smiling as well now.

My heart seems to somersault in my chest every time I say it. Funny. It makes me want to do it again and again and again. I wonder now why I was ever afraid to speak up before.

"Are you real? Am I dreaming?" he mumbles.

"If we are dreaming, then let's never wake up. Let's just keep doing this," I tell him, before grabbing his face and kissing him again. Oh, I love how his beard prickles against my palms. Just like I'd imagined.

I also love how substantial he feels. How his much larger body steadies me, and engulfs me.

Holy shit, I wonder what he'd be like on top? I've waited two whole weeks, what's another couple of hours to find out?

"You're everything I hoped for, Matt," I tell him. "You're *my* counterpart. The one I want."

He groans into my mouth. Desperate, just like how he sounded over the phone. That can only mean one thing. He's so ready. He's on the edge already.

In the background, the faint announcement tells us that boarding has begun. Business class and families with small children first.

I lean back a little to pull away. There's that look. Those brown eyes, pupils so big, they're almost black with desire. He's absolutely gagging for it, as am I. He grabs my waist, pulling me against him. Pretty sure that's not his phone, pressing into my lower abdomen. Must resist.

"They started boarding," I whisper.

"To hell with the flight," he all but growls. "I don't care."

I take a deep, unsteady breath, but I resist the urge to take the bait. "You should care. Because it's waiting to take us home. And once we get there…"

I glance down, at where our bodies are still pressed up against each other. How I wish to reach out and take him into my hand. How I wish to find out if he exceeds my expectations down there as well. But I resist that too.

"Once we get there…" he repeats.

"We'll do every last thing we've fantasized about. Every. Last. Thing," I breathe.

The look on his face is everything. He might have kissed me first just now, but I'm back in the lead again. The time for words is almost over. As soon as we get home from Gatwick, I'll get to do what I do best.

Take action.

HOME

The flight passed so quickly, I barely have any memory of it. Same goes from the train ride across South West London to get to his place. By the time we make it to his front door, we're both so desperate, we all but throw our luggage down on the floor and carry on from where we left off at that empty airport gate. With our mouths and hands all over each other.

In a whirlwind, we barely make it to the couch, where I end up on my back with Matt towering over me while kneeling between my legs.

The look on his face is everything. Everything I could ever hope for. So full of need and desperation.

I've seen lust before in a man, obviously. But this isn't that. Or at least not just that. This is a deeper need. This is one lonely heart crying out to another, rejoicing in the knowledge it's found its missing piece. I know that's what I am to him, because that's what he is to me.

If it wasn't for him, I don't know how I would have made it through the past two weeks. I would have lost my mind for sure. But instead, I've gained so much. What could have been a terrible experience turned out to be something I'll be eternally grateful for. The quarantine that ended up changing my life for the better. *Our lives.*

"I love you, Matt," I whisper, just before he leans down for a kiss.

"I love you," he mumbles against my lips.

"I'm never going to let you go," I tell him, while fisting his hair with one hand, and pulling him down onto me from his waist with the other. He really is quite substantial. Quite thick at the waist, as well as around his thighs... All over, actually. A bear of a man. And yet an absolute sweetheart.

"Me neither. Ever."

He slips his hand into my jacket and pushes my t-shirt up from the bottom. Big, strong hands, just like the rest of him. He makes short work of my top, pushing it out of the way, while I tug at his shirt, exposing the lower half of his torso just in time for our bodies to make contact.

Holy shit.

He never should have worried about his appearance or his size. He had no reason to. I've barely seen much of him, but I'm already convinced. He's the sexiest man alive. *My* man. My world.

"Matt, baby," I moan, while letting my hand travel around his waist towards his ass. Jesus Christ. He has some serious junk in the trunk! And I absolutely love it.

He seems to love my hand there too, because he's grinding down into me now, transferring more of his weight onto me and squishing me into the soft cushions of the couch. The rock hard bulge in his jeans is hitting all those spots which could drive me crazy. If only there weren't so many barriers between us!

"Matt!" I call out, my fingers threading through his hair again.

"Yes, gorgeous," he growls.

"I can't wait," I pant. "I want you!"

He kisses me firmly, as if to show his agreement. It makes me forget my train of thought for just a second. But it all comes back to me when he grinds into my crotch again, awakening all those nerve endings which have only known my own touch lately.

"Matt!" I urge, once I can think again.

"Mhm?" He looks down at me, eyebrows pulled together.

"Clothes," I whine. "Too many clothes!"

He bites his bottom lip, while staring down at mine. He can't get enough of me, just as I can't get enough of him. All the more reason to take this to the next level.

"Clothes off," I say. "I want to see you. *Feel* you."

He tenses, just for a second, while his gaze drops down at himself, then back to me.

I can see that he wants it, just as much as I do. But

again, this isn't just animal lust. We're not just working towards a much needed orgasm here, but so much more. The end goal is the full fairytale. And they lived happily ever after.

And we will, but first, I need for him to take me.

"Sit back. Allow me," I tell him.

He reluctantly gets off me. His shirt slides back down, but not before giving me a tempting glimpse of happy trail. He has no idea how hot he is. No clue. I'm going to have to convince him. By showing him. By loving him.

I rush to take my top off while he settles down in his seat. He stops fumbling with his belt when he catches a glimpse of me wiggling out of my skinny jeans, before kneeling down on the carpet in front of him.

This bra and panty set wouldn't have been my first choice to seduce the man of my dreams, but at least they match. The way his eyes widen when he takes in the view tells me he probably doesn't really care. I could have been wearing rags, and he'd still devour me with his stare.

As would I. But rather than rags, I would prefer nothing at all.

I take over where he left off, undoing his belt, and then the button of his jeans. He shifts his weight, allowing me to pull them off his legs. Neither of us says a word now. The only soundtrack to this moment is the fabric, sliding across bare skin, and our relentlessly shallow breaths, syncing up while fighting for oxygen.

My efforts are rewarded with a glorious view of thick thighs encased in stretchy, tight boxers. The heat coming off him is addictive. I run my hands up his shins, knees, thighs… Waiting for me at the top, a most precious reward. His cock is straining against his shorts, begging to be released. I'm itching to touch it. To caress it. To grab onto it.

But first…

I get up and straddle him, while yanking at the bottom of his shirt and slipping my hand in underneath. He sighs loudly, just like he did that first time over the phone, while his eyes snap shut.

"Matt, you are…" I caress his belly, his sides, his chest, scratching my fingernails across his skin ever so lightly. "God, you're so sexy, Matt!" I tell him.

It's not unexpected, and yet it is. Maybe more so for him maybe, considering how he's looking at me now, disarmed and almost vulnerable.

"You're everything I dreamed of and more," I tell him, while pulling his shirt up and over his head. There he is. My man. In full glory. Well, almost, he's still got his boxers on.

Just like when I first saw him at the airport, I'm in awe.

I trace my fingers through his chest hair and up

and down the hills and valleys of his torso. He's soft, yet powerful. Rugged as well as beautiful. He's a work of art, and he's all mine for the taking.

His body reacts like a dream—my dream—too. Goosebumps appear in the wake of my touch. Although my caresses seem to tickle him, he still seeks them out, leaning in, only to tremble wherever we make contact.

He takes my breath as well as my words away.

And then…

Then he touches me too. His large hand rests on my knee, just for a second. He holds his breath when he lets it travel upwards across my thigh before pausing on the crease of my hip and squeezing me more firmly.

I lean down, nuzzling the center of his chest. Shit, he smells so good. I plant a trail of kisses towards his nipple, before licking and nibbling it like I imagined so many times already. Tastes amazing too.

He bucks up into me, his hand now eagerly grabbing my ass and dragging me up and over his crotch before wrapping his arms all around me.

I can't suppress a squeal when his erection presses up into me. Hell yes. Right there.

In his embrace, I feel safe. At home. And desperate for more. I let my hands roam across his body. I'm not teasing anymore; now I'm just claiming what's always been mine.

Dad bod perfection awaits wherever I touch. I could climb him like a tree. I could stay here forever, wrapped up in his arms; two bodies, quite different in every way and yet so very compatible.

Almost purely on instinct, I start to grind my hips into him, rubbing his solid length against my crotch. It's delicious, even through our underwear. And it's making me greedy for more.

I lean back again to admire him. His broad chest, covered in straight brown hair, just like his beard. Better than even the most tempting dream. He looks up at me full of expectation, or is it admiration? Whatever it is, it mirrors exactly what I hope to express.

Because this moment is everything we wanted, everything we've yearned for. It won't be long now before two become one. I reach back to unclasp my bra, carefully watching his expression when he sees my body come fully into view.

I know that look. The one men get when they want nothing more than to grab what they see.

"Touch me," I whisper.

He hesitates just for a second, but then his right hand lands softly on my breast.

"Taste me…"

His lips are magic, and so is his tongue. He starts off carefully, almost religiously, encircling my areola with just the tip. Round and round he goes, until he plants his mouth around my entire nipple and sucks ever so gently, sending jolts of pleasure straight into my core.

Suddenly I can't stay quiet any longer, moaning desperately in an attempt to egg him on.

Any more of this, and I'm not going to last! What if, what if, what if… He did this *down there?*

I shudder and squirm at the thought. Because as big and strong as he looks, my man has a deliciously light touch. All my previous lovers needed to be reminded to slow down. To touch me more softly. Not so with Matt.

He's taking his time, lavishing attention on my nipples one after the other so thoroughly and sweetly that I'm becoming the one more eager to rush ahead.

Is this what things are going to be like between us? Will I be the one to orgasm almost before things even begin, whereas he'll last way longer?

I can feel it already, building up. My heartbeat and breath rise in feverish anticipation. My skin turns clammy and my voice hoarse as I carry on grinding down into him, in equal parts grateful but also frustrated by the steady pace of his lips.

No. Not like this! I don't want my first orgasm in his presence to be this… one-sided.

I want to feel him completely. Inside and out.

"I'm… sooo… close!" I pant.

He groans into my nipple, which vibrates and

tickles and almost feels even better than when he was just sucking on me. A tingle, deep down in my lower abdomen, makes itself known. Like a sprouting seed, ready to grow into a roaring orgasm if I give it a few… more… nudges.

My eyes wide open, I pull away, roughly forcing my panties down my hips. He watches with bated breath as my pussy comes into view, his hand already inching closer to his shorts.

"Show me," I tell him, my eyes fixed on the treasure I have yet to witness.

He grabs himself; his eyes snap shut when he pumps himself once, before nudging his boxers down just enough to fulfill my demand. His cock is as glorious as the rest of him. Thick and strong, and all mine.

I wish to worship it with my hands, my mouth. Maybe another time, because right now I just can't think beyond one simple desire. I must have him inside of me. To ride him while I cum.

I get back on top of him, wiggling and coaxing to get it in. He's big, or am I small? Not in a way that will hurt me, but just to really let me feel it, satisfying my need to be filled by him.

He lets out a deep groan when I lower myself all the way, trembling and whimpering as my body adjusts to accommodate him. And that's it. Enough to flip a switch somewhere deep inside.

I move on autopilot, my hips bucking up and down, slipping and sliding on his beautiful cock.

"Fuck, Irina, I can't–" he growls, while digging his fingers into my hips, forcing my rhythm even faster.

Patient and kind though he seemed earlier, a different man awakes between my thighs. A rougher, more primal sort of creature. And my body responds, because he's awoken that same instinct in me too. I shut my eyes and focus, taking in every sensation coursing through me.

How on the downward stroke, my clit makes contact with his pubic bone just right. And on the up, his shaft drags across my entire opening, lighting up every nerve ending along the way until I'm fully alive.

Again and again and again. Pressure builds and multiplies. I can't catch a breath, but I don't need to. I just need him. I've always needed him.

"Ohhh!" I cry out, covering my mouth with my hand to muffle myself before it turns into a scream.

"Marry me, Irina!" he demands, while bucking up into me, sending me flying into bliss just as he turns rigid and still.

"Hell yes!" I say. Marry this beautiful man? Could I be so lucky? My body shivers and trembles as dopamine floods my veins. A hot flush of sweet pleasure engulfs me like a wave. I collapse on top of him, still feeling like I'm floating.

"Yes," I repeat. "Yes…"

His arms surround me, grounding me. I'm wrapped up in a blanket of safety and love, listening only to the urgent beat of his heart, competing for attention with my own. This is it, everything I've ever needed. No matter where we might be in the world, this is home.

Seconds, or hours later, Matt clears his throat. The familiarity of it makes me smile into the crook of his neck. "I mean it," he says.

I lean up on one elbow and gaze into his eyes, which are already waiting for me, wide and a little uncertain.

"So do I," I say.

"Marry me, Irina."

"Yes, of course, just…" I lose my train of thought when I start counting the bright amber spots in his otherwise dark brown eyes. Like stars, they are.

"Just, what?"

"Are you asking me to move in with you too?" I wonder aloud, smiling when I spot a red love bite on the side of his neck. I've marked him as my own, without even realizing it.

He pauses for a second.

"Well, I suppose, yeah… Although I hear Edinburgh is pretty nice too," he says.

"I want you to know…" I say.

His eyebrows pull together in a thoughtful frown, which makes me smile even more.

"...I'm happy to live anywhere, as long as it's with you. Even an airport hotel."

The most adorable crooked grin plays on his lips. "I think we can do better than that."

"Don't get me wrong, better is awesome. But worse is okay too," I clarify.

"For better or for worse?" he mumbles.

"Yes," I repeat. "Forever." When it comes to him, it's always going to be a yes for me.

He reaches for my face, and coaxes me down for a tender kiss. "Sorry, I don't have a ring yet."

My chest wells up with so much happiness, it might just explode. Still, I can't stop. I can't get enough of these kisses.

"Didn't find one at the duty free?" I mumble against his mouth.

He briefly shakes his head. His lips barely leave mine for a second. This is it for the rest of the afternoon. This is where we stay. Entwined and naked on the sofa. Kissing and caressing and whispering sweet nothings to each other.

When our bodies grow sore and tired, we go straight to bed. There's no one to disturb us. No Health Check Guy to call us. No buzzer to announce the arrival of food. There's just us. Cocooned in a bubble of love, catching up on all those things we could only talk or dream about lately. Until the sun goes down and the city grows quiet. And we do the one thing we couldn't simulate over the phone. We fall asleep.

Day zero is over. The countdown has reset. Tomorrow will be day one of the rest of our lives.

MATT'S LAST NIGHT OF QUARANTINE

This is a stupid, stupid idea. I definitely shouldn't. I should put the phone down, and try to catch a few hours of shut-eye before the big day tomorrow.

I let my finger hover above the 'submit' button for a painful few seconds, but then I give in to temptation anyway. As I knew I would. Impulse control has never been one of my strengths.

Google's top results for 'Irina Kowalczyk Edinburgh' are unmistakably her. I knew it. I knew it deep down when I teased her during our whole 'love is blind' discussion. She was always going to be pretty, but a part of me is still shocked at what I'm looking at here.

She's the most beautiful woman I've ever seen.

Possibly the most beautiful woman on earth.

Of course I was always going to feel that way about her, but I didn't expect it to be so... Literal. My palms grow so sweaty, I need to wipe my hands before being able to operate the phone again. My heart, which was racing uncontrollably earlier, seems to have sunk into my stomach.

She's everything I could ever have dreamed up and

simultaneously everything I was afraid of as well.

Irina, *my* Irina, from room 203. Wavy blonde hair, slightly tousled as if she'd just spent the day at the beach. Sun-kissed skin, full lips, the cutest little button nose, and a pair of radiant green eyes which would probably turn me to stone if I dared to stare into them for too long.

And she's smiling, which is even more deadly.

I catch myself holding my breath, when my chest starts to feel tight. That's when I exhale again.

Good lord, why? Why do I do this to myself? Why did I let myself fall into this trap?

Suddenly, all those fond memories of the two of us teasing each other, getting each other off in all sorts of ways over the phone take on a whole new meaning. Suddenly, I have a mental image to go with them.

And I can't stand it.

Why did I do this? What did I hope to achieve?

I told myself I was just curious. And that I would just take a quick peek and go to bed. That was a lie. I was trying to prove something to myself.

I was lying in bed, staring at the dark, wondering if come morning, I'd end up making a fool of myself. If everything which developed between the two of us over the last couple of weeks would suddenly turn to shit. And now, Google has answered that concern in the worst possible way.

I should have listened to my early instincts. Distance relationships never work. Going in blind after getting your heart involved is always a terrible idea.

Because there's more to attraction than pleasant conversation. There's more to… love.

Shit, that's what this was, right from the start. Right from the first time she called me, and I heard the painful edge in her voice when she told me in not so many words how lonely she'd been. She awoke a powerful instinct in me.

That little quiver in her voice called out to my entire purpose as a man. To be useful; to be needed; to keep her safe and make her happy. Right then and there, she could have asked for anything, and I would have done it.

What fucking great timing to realize the depth of my feelings for her, right at the very moment it's all fallen apart! Because no matter what she's been telling me, what we've been telling ourselves, this thing between us is hopeless.

She's everything to me. A fantasy, a dream. And I'm… I'm not for her. I'm nobody's dream.

I wasn't anything back in the day either, but at least I was in my prime. Younger, fitter, less jaded, and a few pounds lighter. And I still wasn't any girl's dream, as I learned the hard way when I put myself out there, again and again.

Now, I'm heading quickly towards middle age with the first gray hairs and crunchy knees to prove it.

Some guys make up for that with ambition and drive. Some guys break free from their inherent place in the hierarchy by climbing the corporate ladder and padding their bank accounts. I haven't even done that.

I mean, I'm doing well enough with my mechanical engineering degree and stable career, but I'm hardly a millionaire. It's certainly not enough to overcome the mismatch between the two of us. Far from enough to make her *choose* me, rather than simply settle.

My eyes burn when I squeeze them shut. A deep breath and moment of reflection later, and I manage to regain my composure. I guess I succumbed to temptation for a reason. All these revelations I'm having serve a greater purpose.

Rather than blindly rush towards my own demise tomorrow, I have a chance to prepare, to mitigate the worst of it. I get to change the future, because I'm the only one who can see the disaster looming ahead.

I should ask her to marry me. Make a commitment. Like a proper man. I shake off the thought as soon as it forms. No, that's fucking stupid and would make things even worse!

Right now, I have the opportunity to protect the both of us from a whole lot of future heartache. I just have to be smart, and control my impulses for a fucking change.

Rather than charge ahead, throwing caution and good sense in the wind, I need to take a step back and be sensible. I need to pull the plug on this, before we find ourselves in a hole I can never climb out of again.

I say 'we', but I mean me. She might have convinced herself that looks don't matter. Her intentions might be completely true. And she might even succeed and make herself like me tomorrow.

We might fall into each other's arms, hug, and perhaps kiss. She might feel the excitement and the butterflies and assume that all is well. Best case—or perhaps worst case—she will have convinced herself of her feelings for me so well that even she doesn't know she's faking. I might not be able to tell either. It'll all be great. We'll meet like star crossed lovers, heading straight for their fairytale happy ending.

And then… I'll depart on my flight to London, and she'll go on her way to Edinburgh, and the sheen will wear off. Maybe she'll meet an attractive guy while out with her girlfriends a couple of months from now. Maybe a new colleague joins her team and they hit it off. Suddenly, she'll feel things that weren't there for her with me. And this thing between us, this two-week fantasy, will fade away. Eventually, she'll stop remembering what she liked about me in the first place.

I blink into the darkness, trying to force my eyes to quit stinging. But they don't. None of it stops.

It wouldn't be her fault. It wouldn't be mine either. It would just be… life.

And maybe we'll discuss it like sensible adults, and she'll explain that we've just grown apart. In response, I'll tell her very calmly that that's understandable, and I don't blame her. That I wish her happiness, most of all. I'll mean it too, even if I'm dying inside. I do wish for her to be happy. Simultaneously, I'll want to crush any man who even dares look in her direction. Because in my mind, she'll forever be the one for me. My counterpart. Of course I'll never admit that to her, and I'll certainly never act on it, so she'll never know.

'You're such a nice guy, Matt. You'll make someone very happy one day,' she'll say. It makes me throw up in my mouth a little, because I've heard that one before…

I loved her blind, but now my eyes are open. If I go through with our plan and meet her tomorrow, I'll fall so hard, I'll never recover. It'll be like having it all, only to lose it forever. I can't let that happen.

EPILOGUE

It's a lazy Sunday, and I wake up in my favorite place in the world; tucked safely in the crook of Matt's arm, listening to his reassuringly regular breaths. A distant soundtrack of birdsong and sunlight filtering through the gaps in the curtains tell me it must be mid-morning already. It's just as well that we have nowhere to be today, except here. Together.

It's been Matt and I against the world, ever since we came out of quarantine together two-and-a-half months ago.

The past ten weeks have been a whirlwind, in more ways than one. We didn't waste any time merging our lives. I spent the first few weeks with him in London, and then I got called in to a few back-to-back meetings at the office, requiring me to return to Edinburgh.

He followed a couple of days later, after sorting out his affairs, and that was it. Matt loved it so much in my adopted hometown; he suggested we live here together instead. He's even been able to transfer his job across to his company's Edinburgh office starting next month, so it's all falling into place.

During our first night face-to-face together, I told him that I'd be happy to live anywhere, as long as it was with him. Still, I'd come to feel at home in Edinburgh over the years, so having him here on a permanent basis completes the fairy tale for me.

Except for one thing.

I haven't been able to share my excitement with my best friends; Violet and Joyce. And the more time passes, the more their absence stings. Sure, I'd made some casual friends at work, but it's not the same thing.

Matt and I are engaged to be married. I never envisioned having to plan a wedding without my besties by my side, and so I've been reluctant to discuss setting a date for the big day. Who would I even ask to be my maid of honor? That position was always reserved to be shared between the two of them, and now, I'm left without any backup plan.

Matt stirs next to me and sighs deeply. He stretches out his arm, before tightening it around my shoulders and pulling me against him.

"Morning, beautiful," he mumbles, a content smile playing on his lips.

He's adorable first thing in the morning, or any other time of day, really. I steal a gentle first kiss, which he always reciprocates enthusiastically. Except today.

"Alright, what's wrong?" he asks, pulling away from me.

"It's that obvious, huh?"

He shrugs and brushes my hair back behind my ear. It's crazy how attentive he is. I've never experienced this with any of my previous lovers. Most of them couldn't get a hint even if you hit them over the head with it. But with Matt… He was right there taking care of me from the very first time I picked up the phone and caught him on the other end.

"I was just thinking about Joyce and Violet. It doesn't make any sense that they would keep on dodging my calls and messages. I've sent numerous messages on our combined WhatsApp group this past month, and neither of them has even read them yet."

He gently caresses my cheek with the back of his fingers. This move of his never fails to get my heart racing faster and slower all at once. This morning, the anxiety about my unread messages might also be making my heartrate surge.

"Perhaps it's not about you, but about them?"

"You think the two of them had a falling out and didn't tell me?" I think back to the last messages in the group. "You may be onto something. Last I heard Joyce was going to visit Violet in London, and then… radio silence from one day to the next. I wonder what happened."

Matt shrugs again. "Only one way to find out."

"I'd love to, if either of them would answer my calls!" I complain.

He rolls over onto his back, taking me with him until I'm on top. My other favorite place in the world. Who am I kidding? With Matt, every single position has become my favorite. I glance down and marvel at the warmth in his eyes. They seem to sparkle every time he looks at me and I just can't stare into them enough.

"Give them a reason to answer. Something they can't ignore," Matt suggests.

Excellent. I know just the thing.

"I guess it's time, then," I say, while stealing a few more of those kisses I've become utterly addicted to.

"For?"

"For us to become official." I smile

He raises an eyebrow. "Aren't we official already?"

"Of course, and we both know it. But we haven't exactly been shouting it off the rooftops yet."

"Go on..."

"An engagement party!" I say. "Surely, whatever issue may or may not have arisen between Joyce and Violet can't be big enough to ignore me when I announce my engagement? Plus, it'll be an excellent opportunity for you to get to know a few more locals too!"

"Planning to invite lots of people, are we?" he asks, an amused smile tugging at the corners of his mouth.

"Not *lots*lots. Maybe ten or so? We'll book a table at a nice restaurant; maybe something overlooking the water. Let's be all fancy and grown-up about it!"

"What about family? Do we want to include them too?"

I shrug. "Ah, I haven't really thought about it. Just my mom, from my side? She's never been over, so it could be fun to show her around the city while she's here. She anyway loves you already ever since you called her for me on day one, so it's going to be great. What do you think?"

"Absolutely." He pauses for a moment, his expression turning thoughtful like it usually does when we've discussed family before now. As close as my bond with my mom is, his relationship with his folks is quite the opposite. Middle child syndrome or something. He's always felt like they've prioritized everything and everyone over him. Between that and his past relationship experience, it's no wonder he had trouble believing in us at first.

"You know, you have the best ideas," I tell him, while planting another kiss on his lips.

"Sure, except when I don't." He makes a face.

I frown. He keeps bringing that up just to be hard on himself. "I forgave you for that on the day itself. When will you?"

He looks up at me and shakes his head. "It's not

about that. I never want to lose sight of that moment. What we have is special, but also fragile. I came so close to losing all this–losing you. I very nearly threw it all away and I never want to take you for granted."

"So don't. And anyway, I won't let you." I rake my fingers through his hair, just how he likes it. Sure enough, he lets out a deep breath I didn't know he was holding. "I love you, Matt. You're mine and you'll never be rid of me," I tease, kind of. I'm also dead serious. If he needs me to keep showing him that I pick him above everything else, I'll do it. Again and again and again. Not so he'll take me for granted, but so he'll trust that I've got his back just as he has mine.

"Good." His hands travel down my back, resting on the curve of my ass, before giving it a little squeeze. Just like how Ilike it. "I love you more than words can say."

"Okay, then. No more words." I smile into his lips, before slipping my tongue in between to seek out his. His eyes shut when he loses himself in our first deep kiss of the day. Now, we're actually talking. The way I know best. And apparently, he does too. With our lips and tongues; some sound as well. Just not with too many actual words.

His hand explores the rest of my curves, all the way down to the back of my thigh, before travelling inward, in between. With a tactical flick of his index finger, he finds me already wet and pantyless for him. After everything we've been up to last night, I didn't bother putting them back on.

That's how we've been, on the many mornings we've slept and woke up next to each other.

Pillow talk and pleasure, alternating and overlapping until we're ready to face every new day.

"It's going to be so hard once you have to go to the office again," I mumble.

He smiles, before taking my bottom lip between his and sucking on it gently. I love that too.

"Nah, we'll just set the alarm a little earlier," he says. "Who needs sleep, anyway?"

I place both my palms flat on his chest to raise myself, spreading my legs around him as I go. I grind down into him only to find that he's ready too. He's insatiable, just like I am.

" *That's* how much you love me, is it?" I reach down between us, squeezing his erection through the soft cotton of his shorts. I love how he groans and shudders when I do that. Every single time, as if my affections still take him by surprise. I guess he doesn't want to take that for granted either.

"For as long as you want it," he says. His tone makes my insides all mushy. Because I know he means it.

"How about all day?" I ask. "And all night… and then, forever?"

"There's nowhere I'd rather be."

"Perfect," I breathe, while pushing his shorts down just enough to free his cock, aim, and lower myself onto it. "Because I'll never tire of this."

He grins. Seeing him smile always makes me so happy, I can't help but reciprocate. "You seem keen to start our honeymoon."

"My favorite." My eyes shut involuntarily when I start to rock back and forth on top of him. Still, all I see is him. The warmth and vulnerability in his beautiful eyes. His broad chest and arms, steadying my hurried pace, before inviting me back down into a comforting embrace. A pair of utterly kissable lips, waiting hungrily for mine. All of it is still as perfect in my mind's eye as it ever was, and always will be.

Funny how life works sometimes. Somehow, while I wasn't even really looking, I found him. My dream guy. My one and only counterpart.

AUTHOR'S NOTE

Thanks so much for reading *Blindly in Quarantine!*

Perhaps you've been following me for a while, perhaps you're new to my work. But now that you're here, I'd like to give you a little background on how this book came to be...

My writing career started all the way back in October 2012 when I took a very deep breath, closed my eyes, crossed my fingers and even my toes and clicked 'Publish' on my first short story. That steamy little piece called *Ladies' Day*, and the book it grew into eventually (Beautiful Stranger), are still relevant today because it features a curvy heroine and her more mature lover. It's only fitting that my first ever story was a body positive one!

Since then, I've published a whole bunch of books, in various romance sub genres; as L. Moone I write contemporary, and as Lorelei Moone I write about shifters, vampires and other paranormals. Certain themes tend to repeat themselves throughout my catalogue, though.

Beauty lies in the eye of the beholder. The hang-ups we tend to have about ourselves and our bodies often aren't shared by the opposite sex. While it's a lot more popular to write about gorgeous curvy ladies and muscular alpha males, I have a clear preference for the opposite: dad bod heroes and their admirers. I just never saw many of these books out there. Jessa Kane and her sexy big boy titles, *Hefty* and *Husky*, sparked a change in the romance landscape in 2020. I devoured those books and couldn't get enough. I'm seeing more and more authors enter this space, which is hugely exciting, because I've been writing about plus sized heroes for over ten years now! Finally, our time has come to make this niche more mainstream!

The idea for *Blindly in Quarantine* came to me (predictably) during the first COVID lockdown. A long-distance affair, taking place during a matter of days, between two people who have no way of seeing each other while ironically being stuck in the same damn hotel? Sign me up, please!

Like many of you as well, probably, I was having a hard time that year, though. My creativity suffered a lot, and so I never managed to finish the book. Now, four years later, the world feels like a very different place and COVID has turned into distant memory for the most part. Still, the underlying theme of the story (love is blind), is as relevant as it's ever been, so I simply needed to follow Irina and Matt down the bumpy road towards their happy ending.

To make things easier for you, the reader, I've organised my catalogue into a few different series, which (hopefully) make it easy to find exactly the type of story you're in the mood for. *Blindly in Quarantine* is part of the *Husky Ever After* series; a collection of standalone books which are high heat and high stake dad bod romances. I suspect this series will keep on growing indefinitely, because I'm nowhere near running out of ideas for more!

I also have the *Husky Men Do It Better* series, which contains three interlinked books, each with a self-contained romance arc, but still more fun if read in order.

Finally, if you're in the mood for some curvy ladies being swept of their feet by sexy older heroes, then check out my *Coffee & Curves* series!

By the way, did you know that my books are all set in the same shared universe? Maybe you've already come across familiar names and settings across series, maybe this is the first book of mine you've picked up.

Either way, I hope you'll find all the connections eventually!

And that's enough from me. I hope you enjoyed the story as much as I did while writing it.

x, Lorelei

FIND ME AT:

- ❖ LMoone.com
- ❖ Lorelei Moone on Facebook
- ❖ AuthorLMoone on Instagram

I also write Paranormal Romance as Lorelei Moone. Check out LoreleiMoone.com for more information.

SPECIAL OFFER!

For a limited time, all new mailing list subscribers will receive a FREE short story, called At First Sight.

Claim your free copy here:
LMoone.com
Look for the newsletter sign-up form at the bottom of the page.

www.ingramcontent.com/pod-product-compliance
Lightning Source LLC
Chambersburg PA
CBHW070449170726
48291CB00005B/1664